Monster Baby

BY Dian Curtis Regan

ILLUSTRATED BY Doug Cushman

Clarion Books

Houghton Mifflin Harcourt
Boston New York
2009

Clarion Books, 215 Park Avenue South, New York, NY 10003 • Text copyright © 2009 by Dian Curtis Regan.
Illustrations copyright © 2009 by Doug Cushman • The illustrations were executed in watercolor.
The text was set in 20-point Lemonade. • All rights reserved. • For information about permission to
reproduce selections from this book, write to Permissions, Houghton Mifflin Harcourt Publishing
Company, 215 Park Avenue South, New York, NY 10003. • Clarion Books is an imprint of Houghton Mifflin
Harcourt Publishing Company. • www.clarionbooks.com • Printed in Singapore • Library of Congress
Cataloging-in-Publication Data • Regan, Dian Curtis. • Monster baby / by Dian Curtis Regan ; illustrated
by Doug Cushman. • p. cm. • Summary: Mr. and Mrs. Oliver are delighted to find a newborn baby on their
doorstep one morning, but must learn to adapt when they discover that he is not like other babies. •
ISBN 978-0-547-06006-4 • [1. Foundlings—Fiction. 2. Monsters—Fiction. 3. Size—Fiction. 4. Growth—
Fiction.] I. Cushman, Doug, ill. II. Title. • PZ7.R25854Fo 2009 • [E]—dc22 • 2008039659
TWP 10 9 8 7 6 5 4 3 2 1

For my brother, David Curtis,
who claimed his red-headed little sister was left on the doorstep
—D.C.R.

To Michael and Julie, friends across the Channel
—D.C.

One Saturday morning, Mr. Oliver padded to the door of his farmhouse to fetch the newspaper. But instead of the news, he found a basket covered with a blanket that seemed to be wiggling.

"Wah-wah-waaaaah!"

Mrs. Oliver came running. "Glory, husband! Someone left a baby on our doorstep!"

"Well, of course we'll give you a good home," cooed Mrs. Oliver.

"We will?" said her husband.

"Our wish has come true. After all these years, we've been blessed with a child."

"All I wanted," Mr. Oliver said, "was the morning news."

Mrs. Oliver's hand shook as she pulled away the blanket.

The baby was a tiny thing, sucking one fist, looking like any other newborn . . .

Except for the fur.
The tail.
The pointy teeth.
And the purple horns.

"Oh!" sputtered Mr. Oliver. "It's not a baby—it's a baby *monster!*"

His wife lifted the bundle and cradled it in her arms.

"Well, I think he's the *most* beautiful baby in the world. And he's *ours*," she sang, "tra la, tra la, all ours."

Mrs. Oliver spent the morning sewing diapers for "Olly."
Mr. Oliver fashioned a lemon crate into a cradle until he could build a proper one.

Then he notified Sheriff Grady, but no one seemed to be looking for a purple-horned baby with fur, pointy teeth, and a tail.

Sheriff Grady rode out to the farmhouse to officially proclaim the Olivers foster parents.

Mrs. Oliver was thrilled.

Mr. Oliver wondered why no one seemed to notice that his new son did not look like any other baby in town.

At noon, Mrs. Oliver made jammies for Olly. She carried them to the pantry, which Mr. Oliver had turned into a nursery.
"Glory! Husband, come quick!"

Mr. Oliver did not like being disturbed while pruning his berries, but he rushed to the nursery to see what all the fuss was about.
"Our baby has grown," she said.

Mr. Oliver waited, but his wife did not comment on how odd it all seemed, so he fetched a wheelbarrow to fashion into a larger cradle.

By naptime, Olly had outgrown the wheelbarrow as well as a second pair of jammies.

By dinner, he was crawling.

By bedtime, he was walking.

"Can you talk yet?" cooed Mrs. Oliver. "Can you say 'Mama'?"

"Of course I can, dear Mother," Olly replied. "I can say 'Father,' too."

The next morning, Olly dressed for church in a pair of his father's rolled-up trousers and a baggy shirt.

"This is our foster son," Mr. Oliver told the staring congregation.

Sunday afternoon, Mrs. Oliver taught Olly his letters and how to count to ten.

Sunday evening, Olly read the newspaper quietly to himself.
Mr. Oliver was delighted by how smart and quick the boy seemed . . .

. . . although he did not like sharing his newspaper.

By Monday, Olly had outgrown his father's clothes.
Mrs. Oliver sewed new clothes out of bedsheets.
Mr. Oliver found pencils and crayons. His wife packed a lunch.

They took Olly to school and enrolled him in kindergarten.
"Goodness!" cried Miss Pratt. "He's *much* too big for
kindergarten. How old is he?"

"Three days," said Mr. Oliver, who could not help feeling a bit
proud of his monster foster son.

During the morning, Olly learned colors, shapes . . .

. . . and how to sing the ABC song.

At recess, he played with his classmates.

Or tried to.

After school, Miss Pratt invited the Olivers to a special meeting about Olly. The principal, the nurse, and the janitor came, too.

"What did our son do?" asked a worried Mrs. Oliver. "Did he chew gum? Did he color on the wall? Did he make silly noises during naptime?"

"No," said Miss Pratt. "He was promoted to first grade."

Mr. and Mrs. Oliver hugged Olly as best they could.
And even though it was time to go home and check on his honeybees, Mr. Oliver took the family on a picnic by the lake to celebrate.

Lake Side Park

Olly loved playing with the children at the park.

But sometimes he forgot how much bigger he was.

Olly sighed as he sipped a bucket of pink lemonade. "Being the biggest is no fun at all."

"Oh, but *your father* was once the biggest child on the playground," said Mrs. Oliver as she buttered a biscuit for Olly. "That's how he caught *my* eye. He was always helping the smaller children."

After that, Olly was careful to be gentle with the children.

That evening, Mr. Oliver piled hay in the barn.

Mrs. Oliver made a comfy bed with lots of quilts and pillows.

"May I read you a bedtime story?" she whispered. "About a yellow duckie?"

"No, thank you," Olly whispered back. "I'm reading the encyclopedia. In Latin."

By Friday, Olly had been promoted to fifth grade.

The next weekend, he made the winning touchdown in the big game and graduated from high school.

Three days later, he was awarded a degree in agriculture by the local university.

Olly spent mornings helping his father farm. Mr. Oliver taught
him how to prune berries and gather honey from the bees.
Olly was good with the berries . . .

. . . but not so good with the bees.

Afternoons, Mr. Oliver taught his son how to take top-notch
naps.

Evenings, Olly cooked dinner with the recipes he'd clipped.

Afterwards, the family sat by the fire, sipping tea, and listening to stories and poems Olly had written.

Sometimes, he made up three-act plays to entertain his parents. Olly played every part himself.

On Olly's one-month birthday, the Olivers officially adopted him. They threw a welcome-to-the-family party. Sheriff Grady came, along with Miss Pratt, Olly's classmates, the principal, the nurse, the janitor, the entire congregation, all the children from the park, and . . .

. . . the Ellsworth family, who had just moved into the farm down the road. Olly liked their daughter, Elly, right away.